SPORES

WATER & EARTH: BOOK 01

KATE BREUER

KATE HILDENBRAND

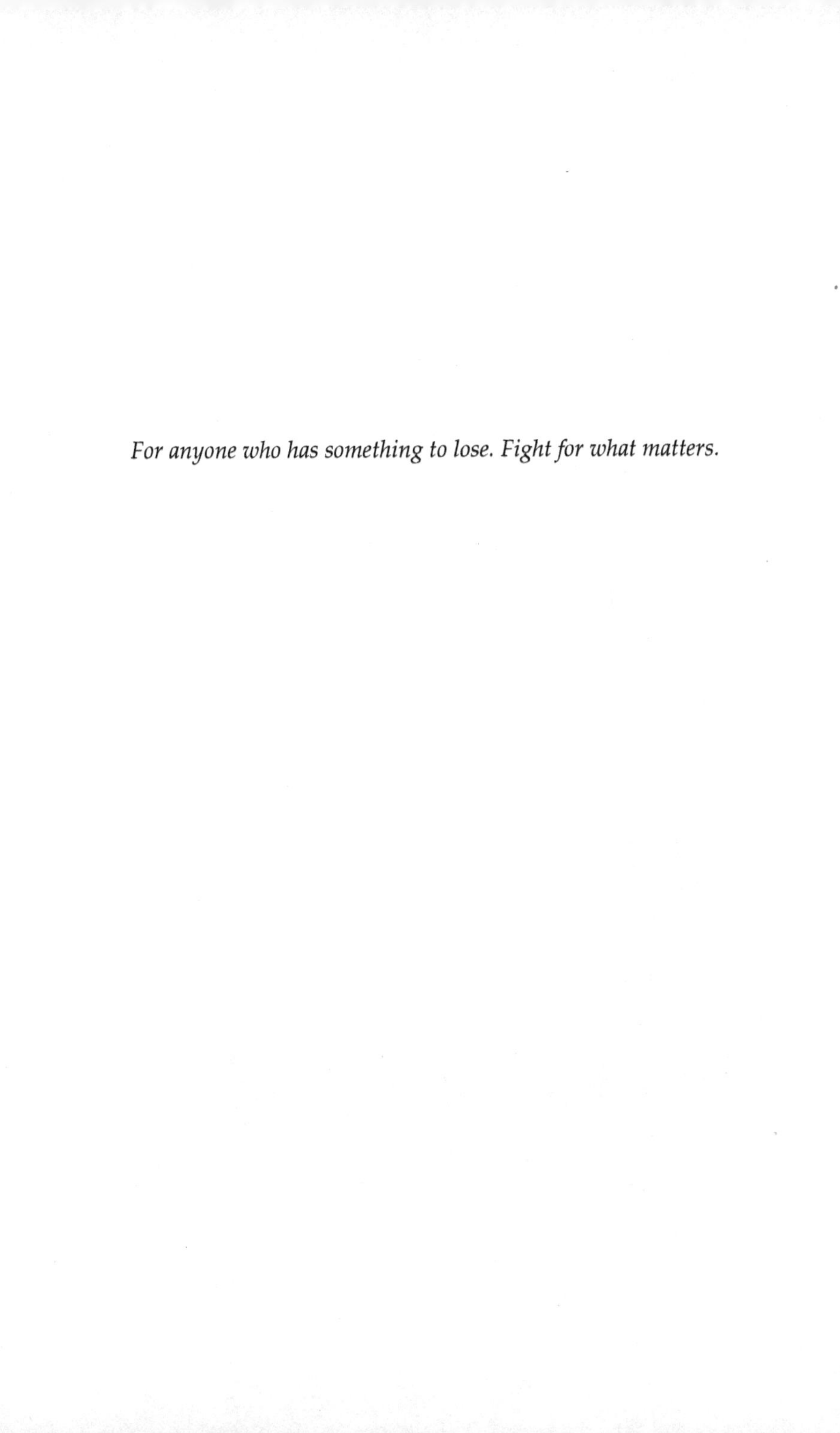

For anyone who has something to lose. Fight for what matters.

CHAPTER
ONE

Arthur didn't know his world would end that day. Eggs and bacon were sizzling in the pan. The toast popped out just when the sirens went off.

"What the hell is going on?" his wife yelled from the staircase, a towel wrapped around her head. "What's that noise?"

The children appeared on either side of her, eyes wide, hands over their ears to block out the blaring sirens.

Arthur sprinted to the front door and peered out. The street was chaos. People ran from house to house. Families carried out their children and luggage. Car doors slammed and cars sped off into the distance. And that was when the panic-derived calm settled in, and he went into automatic mode.

"Kat, get the bags. Pack the essentials. Ron, Erin, grab your favorite toy and get back down here in two minutes."

Without waiting for a response, he turned and stormed into the kitchen. At his touch, cans and packaged food toppled from the shelves into the bag at his feet. Corn. Tomatoes. Beans.

"Kat, where's the fucking camping cooker?"

They didn't usually swear in front of the kids. Today seemed a good day to ignore such self-imposed rules. The kids knew the words anyway. Kindergarten, school, all the kids know them. It was bullshit to pretend otherwise.

He wiped the sweat from his brow with the back of his hand. Too hot. The news had talked about it for weeks. Worsening conditions. No one knows how long. Environmental factors. Too late to save. The only thing Arthur had really noticed was the weather. Much too warm for December. 110 degrees, and not even the slightest breeze to bring relief.

Kat ran down the stairs, passed him, and grabbed the camping cooker from the bottom shelf with trained precision. He would have sworn it hadn't been there when he searched a minute ago. She handed him the cooker and rushed off again, up the stairs, morning gown flowing around her ankles. Her pink-slippered feet were last to vanish from sight.

The car door slammed shut behind his daughter, and they were off. He wished the sirens would stop blaring, or at least blare out a destination. They drove toward town because that was where the majority of cars seemed to go.

Taillights flashing. Honking. Yelling out of car windows. Everything: chaos.

Policemen stopped cars on the bridge towards the city. At this time of the day, there were usually three lanes in either direction. Today, all six lanes were going the same way. He stirred the car along the second lane from the left. Walking would be faster.

At the front of the line, a policeman held up his palm. Arthur pulled up next to him and smiled at the man. Grim military type. Blond stubble visible above a medical-grade face mask. Those eyes didn't smile. A German shepherd sat at attention next to his legs. The man gestured to roll down the window.

"Destination?"

Arthur hesitated. They didn't really have a plan. "CBD," he answered, half question, half statement. "There were sirens to evacuate and we-"

The man raised a thick eyebrow. "Who instructed you on your dedicated evacuation shelter?"

Arthur looked around at Kat. His heart raced. "No one," he admitted reluctantly.

"Please return to your residence until instructed otherwise." The man's voice was monotone, no variance in it at all. The lack of infliction made Arthur angrier than any shouting could have done.

"We can't go home. The sirens."

"Please return to your residence until instructed otherwise." A broken record. Practiced words said over and over.

"The sirens instructed us to evacuate," Arthur said wryly. Semantics. The police officer looked stumped. Arthur almost laughed. Had he found a loophole through this chaos?

"Wait here," the man instructed, and marched toward another officer. A brief discussion. Glances over his shoulder. A raised voice. Confusion. And then the man was back. "Drive to the evacuation center, CBD 1. First exit after the bridge. No discussion. Stay there until instructed otherwise."

The man stepped aside and before anyone could stop them, Arthur pushed down the petal and accelerated out of the control point.

"I'll give him instructed otherwise," he muttered under his breath. Kat gently placed her hand on his knee. She didn't say a word. She didn't have to. Arthur found himself calming down at the mere touch. For the children.

Arthur followed the flow to the first exit. Still no opposing traffic. It struck him as odd, especially after they had almost been made to turn around at the checkpoint. They couldn't be the only ones without instructions.

Signal, check the mirror, turn. There was only one way to go once he took the exit. Police cars blocked the intersection. Arthur turned left, the only option. He slowed down enough to scan the scene. Four police cars. Eight officers, all masked. Two dogs. All military types with no smiles.

Traffic slowed again ahead. Still no opposing traffic. All of them going the same direction, like bugs attracted by light. The lack of choice made him feel tricked, trapped.

The next intersections all showed similar scenes. Forced to turn right, a few blocks straight, another right, then left. He wondered why they sent them on such a detour instead of going the direct route.

"What was that?" Ron gaped out of the window. Nose flat against the glass.

"What was what?" Kat asked with patience only a mother could offer.

"There were people sleeping in the street," Ron explained.

Arthur almost slammed into the car in front when he turned to look at his son. "Arthur, careful!" Kat shrieked, and he turned just in time to slam the brakes.

"Where did you see that, Ronnie?" he asked—without turning this time.

"That intersection we passed… There were people lying in the streets."

Erin strained her neck. "I want to see."

"You can't," Ron explained in exasperation. We are two blocks away. There are houses in the way, dummy."

"I'm not a dummy," Erin wailed. "Mom, Ron called me a dummy."

Kat turned and looked her daughter directly in the eyes. "You are not a dummy, that's right." She turned to her son, the gentleness seeping from her eyes. "Don't be mean to your sister. It is really important that we are nice to each other while we are on this trip, okay?"

She looked from one child to the other until they both nodded, lips curled, sulking. Erin held out her hand to her brother, a peace offering. Ron eyed it warily before he shook it.

With their children appeased, Kat and Arthur exchanged a worried look. Something told them that the bodies in the street hadn't been sleeping.

Much more likely, it was the explanation for the zigzag path they'd been sent on, Arthur thought.

"What do you think happened?" Kat whispered. Arthur cocked his head at the children. "Let's talk about it later."

They followed the caravan of cars to the evacuation center. A woman in a yellow vest directed them into a parking spot. Arthur navigated his car where directed, then opened the car door. "Hold," the woman shouted. He pulled the door shut again. Why was everyone so twitchy?

"Roll down your window, sir," she instructed. Her hands circled the air. Not that anyone still wheeled down a window. Arthur pressed the button. Humming. Fresh air.

"Who instructed you to evacuate to Center CBD One?" she said in a voice monotone enough to rival that of the officer on the bridge.

"There were sirens and we evacuated our home. We—"

"Who instructed you to evacuate to Center CBD One?"

Fuck, no patience, these people. He felt as if he was back in the army. One-sentence answers. Yes, sir. No, sir.

"The officer at the control point on the bridge, ma'am."

He had to fight the urge to salute her. She stepped back.

"Can we get out of the car now?" he asked. She rolled her eyes. He interpreted that as a yes. He swore under his breath, as he stepped out of the vehicle. He let his children out of the back, then grabbed two of the bags from the trunk. Kat shouldered the third.

"Get your things," he instructed the children. Erin jumped into the trunk and pushed Ron's pack toward him. With her stuffed unicorn safely under her arm and her backpack—pink with more unicorns—on her back, she jumped back out of the car.

"You will be required to permit a search of your belongings upon entry of the facility," monotoned the officer.

Arthur didn't answer. He didn't even look at her. Instead, he ushered his children toward the building. Kat held Erin's one hand, Ron her other. Laden with their bags, they walked up to the high rise: office building turned evacuation center.

They stood in line and Kat had to set down the bags. She

rolled her shoulders and massaged her neck. "What the fuck did you pack?"

Before Arthur could retort, they reached the front.

"Name, age, family status," the lean man there said, another uniformed officer. This one might smile occasionally, though he couldn't see his mouth behind a face mask.

"Arthur Reid, 36, married." He indicated himself. "Kathryn Jane Reid, 33, also married; Ronald Dean Reid, 10; and Erin Ann Reid, 7." Arthur rattled down. He felt that any extra words would just get him interrupted again.

"One family?" the officer followed up.

Arthur nodded, his patience thinning. Four people with the same last name, two of them married, two of them children. It seemed obvious to him.

"Who instructed you to evacuate to Center CBD One?"

The same question again. Arthur fought a groan, then repeated, "Officer at the control point on the bridge."

"Welcome to Center CBD One. Please continue inside and wait for further instructions."

Further instructions meant getting patted by officers, each bag rummaged around in, carefully inspected, then moved onto a band next to a metal detector. They were instructed to walk through. Of course, the metal detector beeped when Arthur stepped through. He didn't have anything on him, but it always happened. It earned him another pat down from a grumpy man who clearly thought it was a waste of time.

A small group gathered in front of the elevators. *Ding.* The doors opened and half of them vanished inside.

"I need to pee," Erin announced and immediately started to hop from foot to foot. Even Kat's patience ran thin now. "Can you hold it for just a little longer, sweetie?"

Erin's tip-toe dance sped up, and she shook her head, her teeth clenched. "Mm-mm."

Arthur walked back towards the security check and approached an officer—the first one he could find who wasn't Mr.

Grumpy from earlier. "Excuse me, sir," he started but fell silent at the look he received in return. He shrunk back a little, even before the officer yelled at him to get back in line. Spit hit the man's face shield with every word. He recoiled and returned to his family.

"Sorry, sweetie. There's no toilet here. I'm sure there's one upstairs."

When the elevator dinged again, they rushed inside, a new worry added to their list that only parents could understand. Kat tried to distract Erin with jokes and managed to prevent the worst —for now.

Arthur couldn't suppress a sigh when he stepped off. Another checkpoint. The room smelled of puke, bleach, and death. Nurses rushed in and out of curtains. Blue. The sheer amount of face masks made him feel sick.

Kat approached a young nurse. "Excuse me, ma'am."

The nurse rolled her eyes and rushed away. She didn't even pretend she hadn't heard. Kat tried again with a freckled man. Red hair. Lanky frame. Another Weasley, Kat thought despite herself.

"My daughter really needs to pee," Kat announced without any preliminary hello. She figured it was more important to make someone hear the problem. The man looked up from his tablet. "Not a good time," he answered. Erin's dance sped up. A ticking time bomb. "Well, fine, okay," the redhead added after one look at her. "Follow me, young lady."

Kat set out to follow him but was stopped after a few steps by a palm in front of her. "I'm afraid that's not an option," a heavily muscled guard says. Sunglasses. Buzz cut. The type you'd expect in front of a nightclub. Even his black face mask somehow added to the air of coolness.

Arthur could see Kat's mama bear instinct kick in and reached for her hand. The redhead took Erin's hand. "You can't leave this room until you've been examined. I'm sorry. I promise I'll look after her. "

Arthur squeezed Erin's hand and nodded at the nurse. The

man turned and vanished through curtains. Kat winced when Erin disappeared from view. "It's gonna be okay," Arthur assured her—and himself.

Kat clutched Ron to her side as they waited. Ron objected at first but knew his mother needed him now. He patted her arm around his chest.

"Please follow me." A motherly nurse with a messy bun stepped in front of them. Her arm indicated the nearest curtain.

"We're waiting for our daughter," Kat began to explain.

"I'll need you to follow me. I'm sure your daughter will rejoin you soon."

"Can't we just wait here for her? Let someone else go first?" Kat eyed the place where the redhead had vanished with their daughter.

"I'm afraid that won't be possible," the woman said, still in her caring, understanding voice, but obviously not able to make the call. "There's a line, you know? People waiting to get through."

"Can't we just let someone else go first?" Arthur asked in disbelief.

The security guard with the sunglasses stepped up. "Follow the nurse to your examination, please."

There was no arguing with the tone of voice and before Kat could get them into trouble, he pushed her forward by the small of her back. Kat's eyes didn't leave the small gap in the curtains where she had last seen their daughter until they stepped into the examination room.

Four metal cods lined the walls, two on either side. Metal instruments were neatly sorted onto metal trays. Everything cold metal.

"I'm sorry," the nurse whispered when she led Kat to one of the cods. She looked it. Arthur knew it hadn't been her choice. Kat's expression softened slightly, but her eyes stayed fixed—now on the entrance to the room. No little girl entered.

Arthur sat down on another cod and gestured for his son to sit down on a third. The curtains parted, Kat's eyes lit up, then dulled when two more nurses entered the room. A woman with a sharp nose, whose skin wrapped too tightly around her bones, as if there wasn't enough to work with, joined Arthur. When she stepped up, she pulled up a mask. A little late, Arthur thought and raised an eyebrow. Not that he knew what all the masks were protecting against, but logic said that it was something airborne.

"Where's my daughter," Kat asked, unable to keep the desperation out of her voice. She didn't care what happened to her. All that mattered was that they were together. One family.

"Please, ma'am, let us do our job. You'll be with your daughter again shortly," the motherly nurse reassured her, and while Kat fell silent, she didn't look particularly reassured.

The probing and prodding began. Temperature. Breath. Bright lights on pupils.

"Open your mouth."

"Aaaah." Arthur stuck his tongue out, and almost retched when the plastic stick hit the back of his mouth.

And then they were through. The motherly nurse ushered them out of the room and towards another line. Kat looked over her shoulder, scanning the room for her daughter's vividly blonde head.

The line moved slowly, and it felt like hours passed before they made it to the front. Still no sign of Erin. Kat knew she shouldn't have let her go alone. Arthur hated himself for allowing it to happen. His wife would blame him forever if anything happened to their daughter.

"Name?" The man didn't look up from a tablet, scanned a list.

"Arthur Reid, and this is my wife—" Arthur began but was stopped by a raised palm. "Step through here, sir."

He opened his mouth to object, thought better of it, and stepped through the metal frame. The corridor beyond reminded him of sterile hospital floors. He followed the line to the right, past office doors with eagerly typing men and women in suits. No one looked up as he passed. His wife appeared behind him moments later, shortly after, followed by their son. Ron grabbed his mother's hand, something he hadn't done in years. The surroundings made him feel helpless, like a child thrown into a grown-up action movie. He squeezed tight and let his mother drag him along the brightly lit corridor.

Two women stood in blue scrubs outside a door, both of them lacked the motherly air of the nurse who had examined Kat. Masks stretched over hard features. Eyes expressionless.

"Name?" the woman on the right asked.

"Arthur Reid, Kathryn Jane Reid, Ronald Dean Read. And our daughter, Erin Ann Reid, has been separated from us. She went to pee but didn't come back yet."

To Arthur's surprise, the women let him finish. He was, however, not surprised when they ignored the implied question about his daughter's whereabouts.

"Step through here, sir." She indicated a door to her left. "Take your son with you." She turned to Kat. "Through this door, please." She indicated a door to her right. Kat and Arthur exchanged glances. Erin was already separated, and now they'd be split further. But Arthur knew there was no arguing the point, just like he'd known with the security guard. He grabbed his son's hand and started for the door. Ron clutched onto his mother's hand for as long as he could until their arms were connected by nothing more than fingertips. Then his mother's warm fingers slipped from his grip, and she was gone. Cold air swept past his hand, made him feel alone despite his father's presence. He didn't look away from his mother until the door closed behind him.

Kat found herself in a changing room. Lockers, showers, sinks, toilets. She knew her daughter wouldn't have been able to hold it this long, but at this point she would have preferred her daughter had peed herself than be taken from her. What had she been thinking? She wouldn't have let a stranger take her daughter on any other day.

"Name?"

Kat jumped. She hadn't noticed the woman in the room with her, short Asian lady, nurse's scrubs.

After Kat gave her name, the woman continued the monotone: "Please dispose of your clothes in the bin."

"You want me to strip down here?" Kat looked around. She was alone in the room, but the presence of the Asian woman made her feel watched.

"We'll provide you with new clothes. Please, dispose of your old clothes, take a shower in one of the stalls, and wait for further instructions."

"Can I at least get a towel?" Kat asked.

"You won't need one," the woman stated without sympathy. Kat wondered for a moment, if she was, in fact, human or merely a robot repeating the same instructions over and over. This isn't a sci-fi movie, she told herself.

Another woman entered the room. "Name?," the Asian lady asked.

"Indra Banks, no middle name." The girl's voice was friendly, almost cheerful. "Please dispose of your clothes in the bin," the Asian lady repeated, now facing the newcomer. Teenage girl, maybe 18, if that. The girl shrugged and took off her shirt. No bra. Perky little breasts. Nipples stiff in the cold air of the room. Kat couldn't help but stare at the readiness to undress.

The girl shrugged again, "It's just skin. We all know what bodies look like."

Kat laughed and something loosened in her. She began undressing, next to the girl, until they both stood naked in the foreign room. The Asian woman watched emotionless. "Step into a stall, please."

The girl strode past Kat in determination, opened a shower stall, and vanished inside. Kat picked another one. As soon as the door closed behind her, she could hear hissing from the stall next to hers. Before she could do more than look around in surprise, the shower in her stall turned on. A strong bleach-like smell filled the air. Cold liquid hit her skin. She winced when it touched her. It didn't hurt or sting but made her skin feel raw, as if the water had removed the outer layer. The shower turned off, then turned on again. Hot water—or at least that's what Kate hoped it was—poured out and over her body. The temperature was perfect, and she turned to wash off whatever the first bout had been. The water smelled clean and fresh. A hint of pine cone, maybe. When the water turned off, she looked around for a towel automatically. She pushed the door, but it didn't budge. Panic rose inside her, and when air blasted out of slits in the wall, she shrieked. The girl in the stall next to hers chuckled. "Relax, woman, it's just air. Blow-dryer for your body."

Kat forced her body to relax, even raised her arms to dry off her armpits. The look of the door clicked, and she made herself count to three before stepping out. Can't seem desperate. She found a towel for her hair—not quite dry, a brush, and clothes in the locker across from her shower.

"See, that wasn't too bad," the girl said, a grin on her friendly face. She didn't need a towel, her short black hair dried by the stream of air. Kat envied the lack of maintenance as she brushed her hair and toweled it dry.

The clothes provided were simple but fit well. Cotton sweats, tank top, hoodie. They would do. The girl held out a hand, "Indra Banks." She was wearing the same clothes Kat was. The white tank top seemed even whiter against the girl's dark skin.

"Kathryn Reid, Kat" she answered. "You all alone?"

Indra shrugged again. "Parents died years ago. I'm used to it."

There was no hint of sadness in the dark brown eyes. Kat admired the strength in the girl. "Have you seen a young–" Kat started, but a beep by the door drew their attention.

"Put these on and step through," the Asian woman instructed, holding out two face masks. Kat had forgotten about her.

"Shall we?" Indra asked and led the way to the door while fixing the light blue mask over her mouth.

CHAPTER
TWO

Arthur's scratched his arms where his skin itched from the shower, and he wondered again what had been in the water. Even more, he wondered why he blindly followed every instruction given to him, only to realize that he hadn't really been given a choice since reaching the bridge. There had been police cars blocking all alternate routes, and the reactions to even the lightest objection—fuck, even to too many words—made him certain following instructions wasn't really a choice.

"Dad, everything itches," Ron complained at his side. His responding, "I know, Ron. I know," was perfunctory, but Ron knew there was no point in complaining. As they stood in line for what felt like the hundredth time, he strained his neck, danced on his toes, scanned the room for any sign of his family. With every face—well, the parts visible around the masks—with every head of hair, his hopes sank a little further.

On the other end of the room, Kat was also scanning the crowd, searching for her husband, who was nowhere to be seen. The young woman, Indra, still stood beside her. She had expected her to leave and rush off as soon as they got through the door.

"Ma'am." A tap on her knee. She looked down to find Erin's round eyes looking up at her. Relief, endless relief, flooded her, as she picked the girl up and showered her face in kisses. Her daughter was also wearing a mask, though hers was pink and covered in princesses.

"Mom," Erin objected, "You're embarrassing me."

She held her a little further away and inspected every inch. Unharmed. Whole. Happy. She turned to find the red head still waiting. "I'm sorry it took so long. I had trouble locating you when you were no longer in line at the examination rooms."

"We weren't allowed to wait," Kat stated simply. She didn't feel like explaining herself to the guy.

Then Kat realized that her daughter was wearing the same cotton clothes everyone else was. "Who took her through the showers?" For an uncomfortable moment, she thought the man had, but the embarrassment at the mere question was obvious on his face. "A nurse helped her. I waited outside. I just wanted to be the one to return her to you. I gave you my word and wanted to see it through."

His face was red and his voice flustered. Kat felt bad for even thinking he might have pried on her daughter. The world was a horrible place to produce such thoughts. "Thank you," she said more gently, "I really do appreciate it."

"I'm sure you were worried." The man held out a hand. "I must be off, return to my station."

She shook his hand, muttered another thanks, and watched him vanish in the crowd. And then she saw Arthur. How could she have missed him before, with his head towering above the crowd?

"Hello, cutie," Indra said behind her and waved at Erin. Kat had forgotten she was there.

"Indra, I see my husband over there. Would you like to come along?"

Indra smiled and gestured that she would follow. Kat took large strides along the room, Erin still clutched to her side, until she reached her husband.

At her touch, Arthur turned, his face full of worry. His eyes lit up and his frown disappeared when he saw both her and his daughter in one piece. "Look who it is," he said to Ron, who stood by his side. At least, the family was reunited.

"This is Indra," Kat introduced, "Indra, this is my husband, Arthur, my son, Ron, and you've already met my daughter, Erin."

The girl smiled. "Very nice to meet you, sir." The respect in her voice surprised Kat. Indra hadn't seemed the type when she undressed so boldly.

"Nice to meet you, too," Arthur responded, nudged his son. "Say hello, Ron."

Ron reached out a hand, muttered a shy, "Hello," and returned his gaze to the ground. He wasn't one for strangers. Curious to the point of nosiness once he felt comfortable but shy whenever he met new people. He would meet many new people, Arthur thought. If any of the reports were to be believed, this would be the beginning of a new world, new routines, new people, new habits.

The room fell silent, when a man stepped up to a podium at the front of the room. Kat followed the gaze of the crowd. Buzz cut, stripes, stars. Some high rank. Arthur would know which one. She had never been good with the organization of the military, a bad excuse for an army wife.

The man cleared his throat, and it echoed around the room, amplified by the microphone around his neck. The crowd erupted into chatter, questions, yells for explanations.

"My sister, she's in Utah—"

"What's going on?"

"What about our things? When can we—"

"—what we want. Why—"

Everything muddied into one big chaotic cacophony of sound, and soon it was impossible to make out a single word. Indra leaned closer. "They won't get any answers like this," she whispered into Kat's ear.

"Silence! Please, settle down, ladies and gentlemen."

It took the man almost a full minute to calm the crowd. When only individual idiots yelled out questions, he began to speak, authority in every syllable. This was a man who was used to getting obeyed. "I'm sure you all have questions. If you allow me to speak, I will address as many of them as I can." He cleared his throat again, flattened a piece of paper on his podium. There was a tablet next to it, Kat recognized from the glow on his face, and wondered why he didn't use it for his speech.

"We apologize for the strict procedures when you entered this facility. They were a necessary precaution, and there is no price too high for saving lives. Evacuation centers much like this one have been set up all along the coast and in many other regions of the United States.

"People are evacuated all over the world, starting with the warmer regions where the effects are most extreme, as the disease spreads more quickly in hot climates. You have all heard the reports. No one expected it to happen so quickly—" He paused, broke off mid-sentence. Hmm-hmm. Kat knew he had gone off script. He stroked the paper again, put a finger on it. "Scientists projected conditions beyond the human body within the next five years. Plans were put into action to prepare for the worst case. Unfortunately, the timeline has changed and conditions worsened faster than anticipated. The shelters have been ready for weeks, but we will need time to prepare the next steps.

"In the meantime, you will be provided for at this facility. It will be a tight fit, but it will be enough. Medical staff will be on site 24/7 to ensure the health of everyone who stays here. Military personnel will ensure your safety. The situation is under control."

Arthur believed him less with every assurance. He exchanged a glance with Kat, whose eyes mirrored his skepticism. He grabbed her hand and squeezed it. Ron stood in front of him, back leaned against his father. Erin was cuddled against her mother, too tired to follow anything around her.

"—follow the instructions of the staff." Arthur hadn't noticed he had stopped listening.

"What's happening out there?" a woman in the front shouted. The crowed yelled agreement.

"Please, let me finish. I promise, I will answer your questions." He merely stood until the chatter died down, then continued in a calm, strong voice. "The situation is under control." Indra scoffed next to Kat, and Kat couldn't help but agree. She didn't feel reassured.

"As I said, centers like this one have been set up all over the country. People are getting evacuated and examined as we speak. The military is searching neighborhoods for those who ignored— or didn't hear—the sirens. They will be rounded up and rescued." Against their will, Kat thought. "You are probably wondering why you were examined and why you had to go through decontamination upon your arrival. We deemed it a necessary precaution to prevent the spread of a disease that has rapidly taken over the country. The warm and moist conditions provide optimal breading grounds for mold and other fungi. One of the fungi mutated—please, let me finish. I assure you, it's not as bad as it sounds. One of the fungi mutated and is infecting humans who inhale the spores. The spore hijacks immune cells and quickly infects the rest of the body.

"The good news is, that the fungus doesn't seem to spread from human to human directly. Being close to someone with the disease, even touching someone, doesn't transmit the disease. However, the spores are easily carried on fabrics, and can be passed on via drop infection."

People scattered, stayed close to loved ones, avoided strangers, as panic spread around the room. "Calm down, people. You are safe here."

Yelling. Punching. Shoving. Arthur was reminded of an Irish bar he had visited when stationed abroad. It took the efforts of two dozen soldiers to break up the fights. Even with their help, there were broken noses, black eyes, bruises, and scratches. Reluctantly, the crowd returned their attention to the general.

"A few ground rules need to be followed to ensure everyone's safety. As I told you, the fungus can spread via drip infection." Arthur prayed to gods he didn't believe in that the soldier with the face shield wasn't infected. Face shields don't work. People had known that for decades. Damn him. "Each of you has been provided with a mask. Wear them at all times, as much as possible. We have examined all of you before admitting you and no one in this room shows symptoms, but early stages are hard to detect, and it is better to be overly cautious.

"You have been provided with sterilized clothing to ensure no spores enter the facility through clothing or personal belongings. Your bags will be inspected and items deemed safe will be returned to you over the next few days. Any food items you brought will be added to the stocks of this facility and distributed fairly. We ask that you be patient while this process takes place.

"If you feel sick or detect symptoms in those around you, please report to the nearest medical staff. Please do not wait to see if symptoms worsen. Again, caution is what will keep us safest.

"Outside these walls, the main cause of transmission has been contact with dead bodies. The spores become readily available and infect anyone who gets close enough to breathe them in. Do not touch the dead, no matter who they were or how much you loved them. They are gone beyond your reach, and you don't want to follow them."

Kat had expected some reference to God or souls, but none followed.

"Next, I am sure many of you wonder what happened to loved ones in other parts of the city or country. A database is being built. Your name was registered upon arrival. Staff will ask you more questions over the next days to create a full list. They will need to verify your identity, if at all possible, to ease the process. Once this process has been completed, staff will be able to look up family members and friends in other camps to report on their status. Please refrain from pestering them with questions before the process is complete. An announcement will be made." He took a deep breath, flattened the page "Lastly, all of you will wonder about what will happen next. Over the past two decades, scientists have worked on a solution. We did not expect to need this solution as soon as we do, but it is nonetheless ready. Underwater hubs have been lowered into the ocean. You can imagine them like soap bubbles, giant transparent orbs." Kat was sure the description had been added by an editor. The man didn't seem the type to take the time to explain such details. "The interior has been equipped with the latest technology in air filtration, crop cultivation, and anything else that will be necessary or ease the population of those cities. Hundreds of years ago, our forefathers bested the oceans in search for new land, colonized new worlds. Today, we will be the first settlers under the vast blue sea—pioneers of a new civilization.

"You will be sorted into cities as soon as your registration is complete. Soon after, shuttles will transfer you to the harbor and from there to the hub you were assigned."

* * *

Volunteers weaved through the beds the next day. The same process for every person in the room.

"Name?" an elderly woman in a Tartan dressing gown and a yellow face mask (had they run out of hospital blue?) asked Arthur who was sitting on his field bed with Ron while Kat and Erin sat across from them on another.

"Arthur Reid, ma'am," he answered politely, even though it felt like the thousandth time. He liked the woman, she had been nothing but nice while asking for all of Kat's details and those of the children.

"Date of Birth?" Her voice reminded him of his grandmother —may she rest in peace. He could almost smell the cookies she'd always made for him.

"October 12, 2089."

"And where were you born, sir?"

"Phoenix, Arizona," he supplied. The small house with the red door, so much like their own house in the suburbs. Would they ever see it again?

"Social Security Number?" He rattled it off. Mere days ago, he would have never said it out loud in a room full of people. It didn't matter anymore.

"Thank you, sir. Would you like to be assigned to the same hub as your family?" She had asked Kat and each of the kids the same question. A woman earlier had decided against staying with her husband. They took her away for further questions. From the looks of him, Arthur would have bet anything that he wasn't a nice guy, and she was taking the chance to start a new life. She hadn't returned to her husband's side, but he had seen her around later. She had looked much happier. Free.

The woman in front of him cleared her throat. A fingernail tapped the back of her tablet.

"Yes, we would like to stay together," he answered quickly.

She smiled a sincere smile. "I'm glad to hear that. You and your family will be assigned to the Chicago hub."

"Chicago?" he couldn't help but ask. They were a long way from Chicago. He'd never even been. "Wouldn't something nearby make more sense?"

She chuckled. "Oh, no, sir. Chicago is nearby."

He raised an eyebrow at her. He had never been one for geography, but no one could tell him that Chicago was anywhere near the West coast.

"The Chicago you know doesn't exist anymore." Her voice was sad now. No more smile. "The hubs were named after cities that were—or will soon be—lost forever. This new Chicago is anchored just a few hours South from here."

"What happened in Chicago?" Kat asked from behind the tablet. She had friends there, Arthur remembered. Jessica, was it? He had never met the woman.

"I am not at liberty to discuss the specifics," she answered. When her eyes found Kat's, she added quietly. "I really am sorry."

"What about the people?" Kat stuttered. Arthur had a feeling she wouldn't get an answer.

"I am not at liberty to discuss the specifics," the woman

repeated. She sighed and closed her eyes, as if fighting thoughts. An almost undetectable shake of the head. She wasn't at liberty to discuss, but Kat still got her answer. Arthur wished they could leave, go home. He hated the lack of privacy at the center. Too many people. Too little room. Too much noise.

"I'm sorry, dear," Arthur whispered and placed a hand on his wife's leg. "I'm really sorry."

Kat swallowed hard. A small part of her hoped that Jennifer hadn't been there when it happened. Whatever "it" was. Secrets. She had never liked secrets. To her, they were nothing but lies. Lies of omission. Arthur looked troubled. Something was going on behind those dark eyes of his.

"When are we leaving?" she asked the grandmotherly woman. She knew she would get no further answers about Chicago— probably had already been told more than she should've.

"The first shuttles leave in three days. You will be informed of your exact departure day and time as soon as possible." The sadness in the woman's eyes hadn't quite vanished. The return to procedure seemed to give her comfort, nonetheless.

"Thank you, ma'am," Arthur said and with another sad smile, the woman moved on to the next row. Chicago. She had loved that city. Would the hub be anything like it? She didn't know what to expect.

"Can Tinkerbell come, too?" Erin asked her mother, eyes wide. Too young to understand what was going on. Arthur wondered what would become of the cat. All the pets. He knew some people had brought pets to the compound. He had heard the tantrum of a little boy. "I want Spencer," he had wailed. "Spencer is my favorite. He's a good dog."

Arthur hadn't seen any dogs inside the center.

"I'm afraid not, sweetie," Kat explained. "Tinkerbell will take care of the house while we are gone."

Erin considered this. "Won't she be hungry? Who will feed her?"

Ron opened his mouth but fell silent at a look from Arthur.

The boy was too old to be fooled like that. He knew the cat wasn't taking care of the house. The cat needed care.

"Don't worry, honey. Tinkerbell will be fine," Arthur assured his daughter, avoiding the question. Luckily, Erin got distracted. A few children ran past, giggling and laughing. "Can I go play, mommy?"

Arthur watched as his daughter joined the other children. A small inkling of normalcy in a foreign place. He envied his daughter. Ignorance really was bliss.

CHAPTER
THREE

They didn't get to leave on the first shuttle. Or the second. The center emptied around them. When six out of ten beds lay bare, Arthur began to worry. Kat assured them that they would get their turn soon. Patience. Arthur had never had much of it.

Indra was one of those left at the center. She helped Kat and Arthur with the children, slowly opened up and told them more about herself. It turned out, she was 17 years old, but hadn't grown up in a good home. When the sirens sounded, she left on her own, saw it as her chance to get away from her family. When they asked her if she wanted to be assigned to the same hub as her family, she didn't hesitate to decline. She, like Kat and her family, would be going to Chicago.

More people cleared out over the next days. In the end, fifty people were left at the center. A busload. But no bus came. The volunteers—those that were left—assured them that it was merely a delay. For days, they waited. No bus came.

"What do we do now?" Kat asked him. A low whisper, not to worry the children.

Arthur found the nearest volunteer, a young woman. Black ponytail. Green eyes. Blue face mask. "Is there any update?"

She averted her eyes. A nervous twitch.

"What is it?" he pressed. Something was wrong. He could feel it.

She lowered her voice to barely more than a whisper. "The last transfer into the hub cities... If the bus doesn't get here by morning, we'll have to find our own way." Once she started talking, she didn't seem to be able to stop. Words stumbled over each other. "We can't miss that transfer. It leaves in six days. There's 109 miles between us and the transfer center. One-hundred-and-nine." She looked up at him, her green eyes locking with his. Panic. He lay a hand on her shoulder. Suddenly, she seemed to regret saying anything. "Sir," she urged, "please, don't spread the news. It will create a panic."

Dana had known for days. They had lost contact with the (new) Houston a couple of days ago. "Houston, we have a problem," hadn't helped. The dude who had said it had thought it was clever, funny. No one had laughed. They had a problem and Houston didn't want to—or couldn't—help.

The man in front of her raised an eyebrow. "These people deserve to know. All of us can feel it. We've known for days that something is wrong. Give us some credit."

Dana sighed. She knew he was right. Wished she could tell everyone. Her supervisor had insisted. She hadn't agreed. He wasn't here now, had left on the first shuttle. Save-your-own-ass kind of man—just as she had always known.

"Okay," she said simply. Surprise widened his eyes.

Arthur followed the woman to the podium. She clambered up. She looked scared. Doe in the headlights. "Do you want me to?" he offered, hoping she would refuse. Unable to speak, she nodded. "Would you?"

He waved over some other volunteers, gathered as much information as he could, then walked to the side of the stage, took the stairs up. He stepped up next to her. His hands shook. He clutched the podium. No one below paid him any attention. Some people were asleep. Others talked in groups. A man in the back noticed him, nudged the woman at his side.

"Excuse me," he said, then repeated with more confidence. "Excuse me. May I have your attention for a moment?"

Slowly people gathered. He cleared his throat. His fingers curled around the glass podium, leaving sweaty fingerprints all over it. When the majority had gathered, and the rest looked uninterested, he cleared his throat again. And again. For good measure.

"Thank you," he said. He wished he could have a microphone. "We have been waiting for a shuttle to arrive for days now. Many of us have given up hope. We can't lose hope. I have just been informed that the last transfer into the hub city we've been assigned to will leave in six days."

Gasps. Shouts.

"Who are you?"

"Why did no one tell us?"

"Where's the bus?"

"Why you?"

"What do we do now?"

Panic. He had to prevent it. He had said that the woman should give them credit. Maybe he had given them too much.

"Please, calm down. I don't hold all the answer. Like you, I arrived here when the Northern suburbs were evacuated. Like you, I've been relying on information from those in charge. Like you, I have waited for the shuttle. Like you, I have wondered." He let his eyes sweep across the room. Give everyone the feeling they are included. Public Speaking 101. "We can't lose hope."

As he spoke, the room calmed. People needed someone to tell them what to do. It didn't matter that he was one of them.

"As I said, we still have six days to get to the transfer hub. There are roughly 110 miles between us and our destination. The volunteers suggested waiting until morning to see if the shuttle arrives, but I don't agree."

Muttering. More questions. He held up a hand. It wasn't shaking anymore.

"I believe the best choice would be to leave tonight. We should walk during the night, rest during the day. We have numerous miles to walk. It's hot out there, and it's only getting hotter."

"Why can't we drive?" someone asked, and heads turned toward a man. Midlife crisis suit, greasy hair.

Arthur fought an eye roll, smiled. "Did you see the roads on the way here?" he said patiently. "When we arrived, there was only one way to go. All other options were blocked. There were diseased in some areas. We have to assume conditions are the same elsewhere. We'll go as far as we can." He pulled back his shoulders, "But, we have to plan for the worst."

No one had put Arthur in charge. Arthur didn't want to be in charge. But over the next hours it became clear that he was to be in charge, nonetheless. Anyone with any authority had vacated the center on the earlier shuttles. None of the volunteers knew much more than Arthur and his fellow evacuees did.

In the end, everyone agreed with Arthur's plan. They packed their bags, had a last proper meal, and prepared for a departure at dusk. Indra helped Kat with the packing, while Arthur ran around the room, making inquiries, answering questions, and planning their route.

He asked Dana, the young volunteer, to take him into the parking lot. He needed to see what the status quo was outside. He had hoped that they'd be able to follow the path they had come from for a little while at least. It soon became apparent that wouldn't be an option. While things had been rather ordered when they had arrived, people had been less considerate as things progressed. Cars stood all over the place, blocked entrances, roads. With most of the owners gone, they wouldn't be able to move the cars out of the way. And even if someone knew how to jump a car, it would take hours—many hours, hours they didn't have.

They'd have to walk. At least for now.

* * *

When everyone gathered by the doors, it became apparent that not everyone had been prepared to evacuate. Suits, cocktail dresses, pajamas. Most had backpacks or duffles, but some were less ready for a long walk. Fancy rolling suitcases made for the smooth floors or airports. Crates. Fuck, even a few trash bags. He couldn't blame the homeless. They didn't have a choice. He did blame the rich for not having a plan. They'd soon learn that catastrophe didn't discriminate.

Worst was the footwear. Sandals, high heels, slippers. Not always matching the outfit.

"Anyone know the area?" he shouted when everyone had gathered. A few hands were raised. "Is there a sports goods store somewhere nearby? Outdoor equipment, anything like that?"

One of the few who looked prepared answered. Young man. Hipster-type. "There's an outdoor store just a few blocks from here."

They made it their first stop. Arthur broke the loading dock door. He had learned the skill when he served. Necessary, he reminded himself. Still made him feel like a criminal. He stood by the door and announced, "Everyone, be back here in fifteen minutes. Get yourself shoes, clothes. Remember, this is about function and comfort, not style."

He watched Kat vanish between the aisles, Ron's hand in hers. Indra carried Erin, whispered something in the girl's ear. Erin giggled until they were out of sight. Arthur had grown to like the girl. She was blunt, honest. He appreciated honesty. And she was good with the kids, good for Kat.

As expected, it took more than fifteen minutes. The first people were back after ten, more or less prepared for the 110 miles that lay ahead of them. In the end, they had to round up the rest. Some got distracted by the free shopping, others put too much emphasis on style. Finally, a lot more than 15 minutes later, they were walking.

They had ground to cover.

Arthur led the group, but fell back at times to collect the stragglers. A human shepherd.

He had expected the elderly, the kids, the injured, the handicapped, to be the ones to fall back. They all held their ground. It was the rich and entitled who caused the most issues. They were used to others carrying their weight. Without their fancy suitcases, they had to carry backpacks—heavier than necessary, as they refused to let go of valuables. One woman carried five golden trophies. Some actress. He had never heard of her. These things didn't matter anymore. He hoped she had some other skills to help the new society, but doubted it.

As Arthur circled, Kat walked with Indra. She was glad she had thought ahead, taken a cart for the children at the store. A few of the other families had seen it and done the same. She was grateful. The children couldn't walk as far. They would slow them down. She just hoped the terrain would continue to be good. They wouldn't be able to drag the carts through dirt. And they had wheelchairs and walkers, too. They weren't equipped for tough terrain.

She and Indra dragged the cart together, both children asleep inside, covered in blankets, backpacks for pillows. She envied them, tiredness pulling on her eyes. A nap in the afternoon hadn't been enough. She wished Arthur could stay with her, understood why he couldn't.

With a look around, Kat saw she wasn't the only one tired. Indra yawned widely, quickly stifled it when she saw Kat looking. Indra wasn't one to show weakness. Her family had always considered her weak, someone to shove around due to her size. She wasn't weak. Barely surviving in that household meant she had to be strong. And she would continue to survive. She would do whatever was necessary. And right now, that meant pulling two heavy children in a cart to help Kat, a woman much older than her who she considered a friend by now.

When the sun began to rise, Kat sighed in relief. Surely, it meant they would stop soon. Rest. They needed rest.

Arthur led them into a hotel off the main road. She watched, curiously, as he broke in and opened the main door for them. She had never asked him about his time in the army. She had been curious, but she had never wanted to put him through it. She always thought he would bring it up if he wanted to talk about it. She had said it once, that she was there if he ever needed to talk. He never did.

The lobby was dark, but Kat could still see the bodies in the shadows. When the lights flickered on, she wished someone would turn them back off. The scene was gruesome. They took the stairs to the next level, found empty rooms. Kat insisted that Indra stayed with them. She didn't want the girl to sleep alone.

Arthur slipped back out of the room for a last round of the floor. Just in case. Most groups had retreated into the safety of the hotel rooms, exhausted from their travels and longing for rest and some privacy after weeks at the center. Using only rooms that hadn't been occupied since the last cleaning decreased the likelihood of infection, but Arthur knew some risk remained.

He took the stairs back down to the lobby, found a few fellow travelers at the bar. He could do with a drink. Something strong. Whiskey. Neat. No bartender meant he'd pour his own drink. He picked a bottle from the top shelf. He'd barely had the chance to order top shelf. No time like the end of the world for a good drink.

The amber liquid trickled into the glass. He added two ice cubes. They cracked when they hit the liquor.

He let himself fall into an armchair. A good bar, comfortable armchairs. He understood why people spent money on this shit. A man joined him, took the armchair next to him. "Thank you for getting us here," he said. Arthur nodded curtly. He had looked forward to a drink in peace.

The man folded his legs. "A few of the men and I are cleaning up the lobby before we turn in. Make sure the children don't see the bodies in the evening. We thought you should know. We wanted to make sure you were alright with it."

Relief. Someone other than him taking charge, even if they cleared it with him. "I think that's an excellent idea. I'll join you in a minute."

If he could just get a minute.

"No, sir, no. You've done enough for today. Enjoy your drink. I'm sure you need some peace and quiet. I'll leave you to it. Then, get back to your family, be with them. Rest. You deserve it."

Arthur smiled at him. A thankful, relieved smile. He would have helped them. But the man was right. He needed some rest. "Thank you. What's your name, sir?"

"Jim," the man answered, returning the smile. "Jim Washington."

"Nice to meet you, Jim." Arthur held out his hand. They shook. As promised, Jim walked away and left him with his drink. He called after him, "Jim." The man turned, an eyebrow raised. "Be careful. Make sure to wear masks, wash up after. Be safe." Another nod, and Jim walked away.

The ice had already melted most of the way. The whiskey was no less good. And he needed the drink.

When he had finished it, he made his way back upstairs. Six or seven men cleaned up the lobby when he passed. Jim waved good-night. He waved back, but didn't stop to talk. Jim was right. He needed to be with his family.

He found the children still asleep, tucked into bed. They would wake up sooner than any of them liked. They should rest while they could. Kat sat in a chair on the balcony, a blanket wrapped around her. When he stepped outside, he saw Indra in another one next to her. Indra had her knees pulled into her chest, a blanket tight around her.

"Is everything okay?" Kat asked in a low voice. He leaned against the railing. "Some people are cleaning up downstairs. For the children. And, I think, for the dead. Give them some respect."

Kat nods. "I was worried about that, about how to get the children out without them seeing. We were talking about that. About what the children might have to see." She looked at him intently. "I don't think Ron will mistake bodies for asleep again. Not after what he heard during that speech. He isn't stupid. None of them are."

Indra yawned. "I think I'll try to get some sleep. I bet the little rascals will be up soon." Mostly, she figured the couple would need some privacy. It had been a while since any of them had been alone. Too many people in that fucking place, even at the end.

Erin had the blanket wrapped around her feet. Indra bent over the girl and tucked her back in. She walked around the bed, stroked some hair out of Ron's face, then walked to the second bed. Without undressing, she slipped under the covers. They had exchanged them for new ones from the linen cabinet, just to be safe.

The bed was comfortable, more comfortable than the field bed she had slept in at the center, definitely more comfortable than the "bed" she'd had at home: a worn-through mattress she had found on the street and dragged into the garage herself. No one at her parent's house had been able to afford a car, so it was more storage room than anything. Her parents had barely ever disturbed her there. It hadn't been much, but it beat sharing the house with her drug-addicted parents and whoever they'd let stay at the house at the time. Drug dealers, people they owed favors— or money.

The world might be going to shit, but her world was looking up. And she would do anything to keep it that way. There were people in her life she cared about now—who cared about her. And for the first time in her life, she had hope. Hope. It was everything.

* * *

The Spores claimed eight people over the next two days. None of them had been on the cleanup crew. No, the men had been careful. Masks, gloves, a shower afterward. The first two who got sick were teenagers. Idiots. They had dared each other to get closer and closer to the dead. They hadn't meant to actually touch them. Drunk on free booze from the bar. Not enough respect for the disease or the dead.

The coughing started in the wee hours of the night. They were dead by sunrise. The Spores killed fast. The next victims were their parents, their siblings. Overcome by grief, they embraced the dead. The Spores welcomed the close contact, settled in. Later, when they removed the masks, comforted each other, the Spores claimed them. Coughing, fever, death.

Forty-two, Arthur thought. Sixteen percent lost. Eighty-four percent still alive, he forced himself to think.

Forty-two people left. Three nights. Roughly 50 miles.

During their fourth night, they made slow progress. Too many cars on the road. Most were empty. Some were not. Kat shielded Erin's eyes when they walked past a car with blood on the window. Four dead inside, Arthur noted.

"We should head for the freeway," Indra suggested. "Even if there are many cars, the lanes are wide enough to walk in between."

Arthur considered it. The girl was right. If motorcycles could fit comfortably in between the lanes, so could people. They headed for the 5. He had always liked the ride down, ocean on the right. Once, he had seen whales in the distance—from his car. He counted himself lucky.

Soon, we'll all live with the whales. Humans, underwater. He shook his head. It sounded surreal. Like something for a distant future.

The freeway had been a good choice. Most of the time, they could follow the shoulder. The ocean brought a breeze. Kat breathed in deeply. She had always loved the smell of the ocean. She had often spent her days off at the beach. A good book. The endless blue. Salty air. Free therapy.

The moon glittered on the waves in the distance. Not a cloud in the sky. It was warm, even at night. They walked. And walked. And walked. When the sun rose over the hills to their left, they turned off the freeway.

They stayed the night in an open-air mall. Many small shops. A grocery store. Beds, couches. There were enough places to sleep. Not as comfortable as the hotel, but it would do. They unpacked duvets, blankets, and sheets. The bedding section held enough beds for most.

Arthur did a last round, then followed Kat and Indra outside and into the decoration store next door. It would have been a nice place to shop, Indra thought. Not that she would have been able to afford even a candle. She smelled a few, and added three favorites to her bag. No one would miss them.

A king bed stood in the middle. She helped them convert it from decoration to purpose: fewer pillows. A comfortable blanket.

She tucked in the children, before she curled up on a sofa. She saw Arthur and Kat slip under the covers, their children between them, and turned to face away. They deserved some privacy. Seeing them kiss made her feel lonely, anyway. Her only kiss had been on a dare. A friend. No meaning. She hoped to find someone she wanted to kiss at some point. Maybe, just maybe, it would be possible in this new life. Less focus on mere survival. Soon.

* * *

She awoke from her dreams, sat bolt upright. A scream? Had she heard a scream? Arthur and Kat jumped out of bed. They had heard it, too. Another scream made them sure. Kat stayed with the children. Arthur told Indra to stay with them, but she ignored him, and followed Arthur outside. Indra wasn't weak.

More screams, shouting. Something was happening at the store. Two men stood outside. Body guard types. One of them held a gun. Arthur pressed Indra into the wall. Instinct took over. He was back in the field. A soldier.

"Stay here," he whispered. Urgency in his voice. He crept toward the edge of the building, into the gap between the decoration store and the large building. Slowly, he edged closer and closer to his foes. They were talking, laughing. Careless, too used to finding easy targets. Before they knew he was there, he attacked. Elbow to the face. Punch to the stomach. The gun was his in seconds. The former owner lay sprawled on the ground, holding his stomach and nose. Blood ran past his fingers. Probably broken.

He pointed the gun at the other man. Angry eyes told him he wasn't ready to give up. "Don't be stupid," Arthur said calmly. "Don't make me hurt you."

Slowly, the man raised his hands. Indra stepped up next to him. He handed her the gun, let his hands linger on hers for a moment. Together, they trained the gun on the second man. "You okay?" he asked, and she nodded. "I've got this."

There was strength in the girl. More strength than a body her size should hold. Or a girl her age. For a moment, he wondered just how bad things had been at home. No matter what forged her into who she was, he was glad she was with them.

"Can you watch these idiots?"

"I've got this," Indra repeated. She kept the gun raised and pointed at the two men. "Don't move."

Arthur hated leaving her there with them, but the alternative was killing them. He wasn't ready for such length. He had to trust her resilience.

He crouched behind an aisle and walked light-footed to the mattress section—toward the noise. As expected, more guns. Three men stood between him and his group, two threatening his companions, one collecting valuables. Jewelry, food, supplies. They were in a market, and he dared take from people. It was cruel, unnecessary. A show of power, not need. He swore under his breath. Three against one. Plus, two guns. And there were children watching. Fuck.

He slipped back into the shadows, back toward the door. There, he waited. Patient. And waited. Finally, the men made their way back to the door. He jumped out at the first, tackled him to the ground, grabbed the gun from his waist. Without thinking, he twisted, turned, aimed the gun at the second man. He lifted himself up on his second hand, swiped the feet out from under the man. Two men down, one more to go. He punched the third in the head, knocked him out. The other two scrambled, ran. They didn't even turn, left their third behind without hesitation. He followed. When he got to the door, Indra had the gun trained on the men. One girl holding her own against four men. With a smile. A devious smile. She was right: she had it.

"Put your gun down. Slowly," she instructed. He waited, ready to help Indra, but not interfering. This was her win. The man put his gun on the ground, his hands in the air. Four men cowering before her. Indra grinned.

"Leave what you took," she said, "You don't deserve any of it." She watched eagerly as they emptied their pockets, their bags, even removed jewelry from around their necks. Greedy filth. Like her father. Want, want, want. They could have asked for help. There was enough food in the market for everyone. They would have shared, maybe even let them join them on their way. She shook her head. Stupid. Greed made people stupid.

"And now run, get out of here, and don't come back until we are gone. I don't want to see your ugly little faces ever again."

They scrambled, ran for the hills. Indra's grin deepened, as she enjoyed her little win. She saw Arthur hover in the shadows. "Thank you," she said. She knew he could've taken over. She knew he would've had an easy time overcoming the men. She was thankful for the opportunity to hold her own.

He returned her smile and didn't object, when she secured the gun and stuffed it into the back of her jeans. He trusted her with it. She wouldn't use it unless she had to. She had proved that.

"There's one more man inside," Arthur said. When she raised an eyebrow, he added, "Unconscious. Knocked him out. But he'll come around, and soon."

She picked up the loot, shouldered the bag, and followed him inside. "We should also check in on the others. They are probably terrified."

He nodded. "How about I take care of the man, while you do that."

She looked surprised. "Will they listen to me?"

He grinned. "I'm sure you can make them."

Without waiting for an answer, he kneeled next to the man on the ground. She passed him and walked towards the mattress section. She found families cowering together, strained whispers, tears. They were scared. When she emptied the bag on a bed, their eyes widened.

"How?" A plump woman asked. Two children cried against her chest.

She grinned. "We thought you might want these back."

She waited while the people recovered their valuables, slipped wedding rings back on, reattached necklaces. No one picked up the food. They could separate that later.

"I want you to know that you are safe here. No one will harm you as long as we stick together. " She drew back her shoulders. "We showed them that they can't just push us over. We are strong together."

They stared at her. No one said a word.

"Get some more rest. We leave at sunset," she finished. No one moved. "I promise you will be safe. We will keep you safe."

"Thank you," the same woman said, her fingers clutched tightly around a ring hanging from a necklace around her neck. Indra bowed her head, then turned back toward the entrance. Arthur waited outside. There was no sign of the man.

"Where did he go?"

Arthur pointed at the hills. She could see a man running for his life, getting smaller and smaller. "My wake-up might have been a little—" he held out his hands in an innocent gesture, "—cold."

She smiled. "What did you do?"

He pointed at the ice machine. "Got him a cold bath to make

him come 'round. When he opened his eyes, he had a gun to his head. Didn't need much convincing after that."

They both laughed, and it pushed away the last of the afternoon's scare. Together, they walked back toward the decoration store. There was strength in numbers.

Two more nights. They could make it. They would make it. Had to make it. Two more nights.

CHAPTER
FOUR

When his watch beeped the next evening, Arthur felt drained. He sat up, blew air through his cheeks, slapped his own face. Exhaustion was pulling on him. It was showing on everyone's faces.

They gathered outside the store. Refilled water bottles with ice from the machine, replenished supplies. Kat handed him an apple. He frowned but took it. The end of the world didn't have to be the end of his health.

Forty-two people set out that morning. The Spores claimed four more before nightfall. No one knew how they had caught it. There was strength in numbers. In times like these, there was also risk in numbers.

Indra kept up constant reminders to not take off the face masks, to not touch the dead. A broken record no one listened to. She understood. The face mask was itchy and felt as if it restricted breathing. She knew she got enough air, but knowing and feeling are two very different things. She scratched through the mask, didn't dare take it off even for a moment.

Erin grabbed her hand. She looked at the girl, smiled. "Are you walking today?"

Erin nodded proudly. "I'm a big girl." Indra had a feeling this new-found motivation was a response to Ron's earlier teasing. He had called her a baby for sitting in the cart.

"A big girl? Yes, you are," she smiled.

Ron was running ahead, catching up with his dad. "How much further?" he asked when he reached his father. Arthur looked around with tired eyes. "We'll get there today or tomorrow," he explained. Ron folded his arms. "I'm sick of walking."

Arthur laughed dryly. "Me, too, kid. Me, too."

Ron looked up at his dad, saw the exhaustion. He took his father's hand, more to show support than for himself. It was the only thing he could think of to help. Arthur looked down at their hands, smiled. "Thank you for being strong," he said, and Ron nodded.

Arthur scanned the road ahead. He couldn't see far in the darkness of night. It made him nervous. Clouds covered the moon, so it was even darker than the previous few nights. And it was quiet. Quiet voices behind him. Shuffling feet. The squeak of a wheelchair. Or was it a cart? But it was the eerie silence beyond their group that made him uncomfortable.

The city had always been full of noise. Cars, people, stores. There was always something. He used to complain about the construction sites, the honking cars, the loud music of their neighbors. He would have welcomed the silence then. Now, it made him nervous.

There were no houses next to the road, either. Just dirt on one side, ocean on the other.

"Arthur," Kat whispered behind him. He slowed, Ron still by his side. She caught up, and he looked at her. She lowered her voice further. "Coyotes."

He followed her gaze. There was movement in the hills to their left. Hard to make out details. "Can you see how many?"

She shook her head. "At least a handful, maybe more."

It turned out that "maybe more" was still an understatement. Soon after, the coyotes entered the road ahead, their noses low to the ground, sniffing. Arthur held up his hand, stopped. Slowly, those behind him noticed, too, and fell silent. No one dared move.

At least two dozen coyotes slunk through the cars ahead. Coyotes usually traveled in smaller packs. This wasn't normal. He waited, slowed his breathing. They couldn't panic.

The leading coyote raised his head, light catching his eyes. He sniffed, and then he howled. Not the slow, melodic howl of a wolf, but a high-pitched, eerie sound. The others answered, yapping, howling.

The pack stormed toward them. Fuck.

He had relied on them not attacking. Coyotes usually didn't attack humans. They were scared. This pack wasn't. And there were too many.

"Everyone, hide. Get into cars, close the doors. Don't come out."

And that was when the panic set in. A family ran for the hills, scared for their lives. The coyotes hunted them down with ease. The family didn't stand a chance. Four dead. Most of the group managed to hide in the cars. Arthur grabbed the arm of one of a man in a wheelchair, stuffed him unceremoniously into a car.

He grabbed Ron around the middle, searched for Kat, Indra, his daughter. No sign of them. He tried a few locked doors, before one opened. Finally, he locked himself and his son into a pickup. Arthur threw the driver's corpse onto the street. The coyotes devoured him. Blood sprayed onto the window. Ron didn't look scared. His sweet, innocent boy. Just weeks ago, he had mistaken a bunch of dead for sleeping. Now, he watched as coyotes tore pieces of a corpse and didn't flinch. It disturbed him, but his boy's bravery filled him with hope.

"Where are Mom and Erin? Indra?" Ron asked from his lap. He wished he had an answer. They would find them. They had to be okay. The night was filled with screams, with howls and yaps, and then with eerie silence.

The last coyotes were gone by sunrise.

"Stay in the car, Ron. And don't take off the mask. Don't touch anything."

To his surprise, Ron didn't argue. Arthur eased open the door. He tried not to step onto the body. A soft slurping told him he failed. Something gave below his shoe, and the soldier in him took over. Now was not the time for nausea.

With his mask safely in place, he walked through the cars. Group by group, people joined him. Not enough. He kept walking, searched the surrounding cars. When he spotted a vividly blond head in a van, he tore open the door. Erin threw her arms around him. "Daddy!"

He held her tight, looked over her shoulder. Kat and Indra lay in the back. They were okay. Everyone was okay.

A quick headcount showed that it wasn't everyone. His family was okay, but they had lost many to the coyotes. Twenty-seven left. They had lost almost half their group since setting out. Indra looked devastated. "I promised them, we'd keep them safe."

Kat took the girl's hand. "It's not your fault, that they didn't hide. If they had listened, they would be safe now."

Indra didn't look convinced. "I should've forced them."

Arthur looked right into her eyes. "Indra, listen to me. You can't stop people from being idiots. You can tell them what to do. You can help them see the correct path. But you can't force them to do the right thing. It's impossible. If you blame yourself for other people's failure, you will never be happy. You did what you could, and then you did what you had to do. If you had stayed, you would be dead now."

Thoughts bubbled through her mind. Arthur was right. She couldn't have saved them. She nodded, crawled out of the car. "Let's hope those idiots kept their masks on and didn't touch their faces. There were countless dead in those cars."

Dread filled Arthur as he looked around. "Everyone, keep your masks on. Be extra careful what you touch. We'll need to find a place to wash, to change into fresh clothes. Until then, don't touch anything. Don't take off your masks."

A few people hastily replaced their face masks. Idiots.

* * *

They washed at a rest station a few miles South. They left the clothes, no one dared touch them. When everyone was showered, supplied with fresh face masks, and dressed in clean clothes from the store, they rested. They couldn't stay here all day. They had lost too much time the previous night.

The air grew hotter around them, as they ate and drank. Arthur broke open a snack machine and handed out chips, cereal bars, and candy. When the chocolate made his teeth hurt, he was thankful for the apple Kat had given him. She looked out for him even when the world was ending.

Covering distance was important, but the heat worried Arthur. They had children and elderly with them. Even he felt the strain of the heat—and they hadn't even started walking. He waved Indra over. "Can you get me the map?"

She recovered it from her pack and spread it out in front of him on the ground. "It's hot," was all she said.

"It's what worries me."

He traced the lines of the I-5 down to the rest station, tapped the spot. "This is where we are." He followed the coast and located the harbor. "And this is where we need to go."

"How far is it?"

"30 miles, I'd say," he guessed, using the scale in the corner. "We have one more night, but we need to get there by nightfall tomorrow, or they'll leave without us. I'd rather get there early, have some buffer."

Indra frowned. "We lost time last night. Too much time."

Absently, he nodded.

She crouched next to the map. "The city starts here. We should get there before dark to avoid more coyotes. We can't afford to lose more time."

Arthur didn't point out that the coyotes would likely be in the city as well.

Indra glanced at the sky, at her watch. "It's too hot now. Let them rest. We'll leave in the afternoon when the wind turns."

Her initiative and knowledge surprised him. It must have shown on his face. "I've always had an interest in science, especially biology, the ocean. Fishers use the winds to carry them out in the morning, back in the afternoon. It will bring cool air if we wait—well, less hot anyway."

She had a point. If they set out now, they wouldn't make it far. He got up, raised his voice. "Listen up, everyone. Find shade, get some rest. We'll set out again in the afternoon, walk through the night and until we reach the harbor. Get as much sleep as you can. It'll be a long night."

Indra and Arthur's family spread their blankets under a nearby tree. The grass underneath was soft enough, and he soon drifted into light sleep. An uneasy feeling pulled at him like a shadow looming just out of sight.

* * *

Indra's prediction had held true. It was still hot, but a breeze carried cooler air from the ocean, along with a salty smell. Arthur lifted his arms, welcomed the chill that dried the sweat under his arms. A sigh escaped his lips.

The landscape began to shift around them. The outskirts of the city crept up and brought hope with them. They still had a long way to go, but it felt within reach now. Possible.

They walked. And walked. And walked. At first, Indra had distracted them and herself by explaining why the ocean smells the way it does, how the ocean and land cooling at different rates caused the winds, and any other fact about the ocean she could think of. But when her mouth parched and her feet hurt, she quieted.

The outskirts became suburbs, then city. And they kept walking.

He scanned the remainder of the group. They had lost almost half, and those who remained looked drained. Indra put her hand on Kat's shoulder, whispered something. A short nod from Kat and Indra fell back. He walked over to help Kat with the burden of the cart. He knew she could do it, but she looked exhausted. "Are you holding up okay?" he asked when she smiled at him.

"I've made it this far. I'll make it the rest of the way."

He had married a strong woman. He had always known it, but the current circumstances proved it.

Indra slowed until she was at the rear of the group. She had noticed the group spread and thin further, as those toward the back fell further behind. An elderly woman in a tartan jacket leaned onto her walker, several minutes behind Arthur in the lead. Determination on her face, sweat on her brows. A fighter, Indra thought. Next to her, a young man in a wheelchair kept up a stream of encouragements. "Come on, Helga. You've got this."

"How about a short rest?" Indra suggested kindly. "I'll let Arthur know."

The woman shook her head. "I won't slow anyone down."

"I'm sure the rest of the group will appreciate a few minutes. I know how tired I am," she pressed. The man jumped on it. "I'm exhausted. My arms need a rest. All of us do. We are just too stubborn to ask for a break."

In the end, Helga gave in. Just in time, Indra thought, when the woman collapsed onto her walker. She patted her brow and accepted a bottle of water from the young man. Achim, as he told Indra during the break. A look around told Indra that Helga wasn't the only one close to her limit. They had been walking for days—something most of them weren't used to. Her own feet were used to walking, but most of the group was covered in blister pads.

"I should check in with Arthur, see how much further we need to walk." She exchanged a look with Achim. Indra squeezed Helga's shoulder, before she left her in Achim's care and joined Arthur and his family. "People are at their limits."

Arthur grimaced. "I know."

"How much further?"

Kat smiled sadly. "Too far. I'm not sure everyone will make it."

"We still have fifteen miles to go." He pressed the button on his watch to light up the display. "And sunrise is only a couple hours away."

Indra groaned. "This will only get worse. Add heat to exhaustion, and we might as well give up now."

"I wish we could drive," Kat said. There were still too many cars on the road to make that feasible. There might have been a couple of miles here or there in between, but never enough to warrant searching for enough cars to hold them all.

"We should go on," Arthur stated. He looked defeated. "It's our only chance."

Indra nodded. "I'll stay at the rear, make sure no one falls too far behind." Not that there was much she could do if anyone actually reached their limit. She hoped bodily limits were higher than mental limits. Mental limits could be overcome.

Achim turned out to be a champion at motivation. He zoomed between the stragglers and spurred them on. His mood could not be dampened, even when the sun started to rise and heat started adding its own battle. Indra watched him with fascination as he pushed his wheelchair up inclines, around potholes, and through dirt. All with a smile.

Still, she loosed a breath when they reached the bridge that meant they reached their final mile. By the time, they set foot on it, the sun was relentless. She wiped sweat from her face with her shirt. Pointless. New beads had already formed. She couldn't wait to reach the ocean. A swim sounded more than nice right now.

There wasn't a single car on the bridge. It struck her as odd. The streets had been blocked almost everywhere by abandoned cars along the way. A few miles were barely drivable here and there. Barely. The bridge was completely clear.

"Are you gonna be okay back here for the last bit?" she asked Achim. A big grin told her he would be more than okay. She liked the guy.

With quickening steps, she made her way to the front, caught up with Arthur, Kat, the kids. Ron and Erin were up again, walking between their parents. They had been sleeping on and off, lost their schedule. Both looked worn and exhausted.

"Something doesn't feel right," she stated. Arthur didn't answer. Kat looked around at her, tried to read the girl's expression. Indra looked worried, her dark face gleaming with sweat. They were less than a mile from their destination. Kat didn't have any energy left to worry.

"What's wrong, sweetheart?" she asked, even though she didn't want to hear an answer.

"It's too empty here. Not a single car, nothing."

Arthur looked around. He hadn't noticed it. Now that she pointed it out, the lack of obstacles started to worry him as well. He stopped, held up a hand. The group slowed. Worry. Confusion. Exhaustion. Excitement. All mixed on the faces of those around him.

"I'd like to walk ahead with three or four of you. Just to make sure it's safe. Please, wait here." He pointed at two men. "Would you come with me?" He looked at Indra. "You too?"

One of them exchanged a glance with a bearded redhead by his side, kissed him, then joined Arthur. The other shrugged and walked up. Arthur scanned the group. "The rest of you, please keep your eyes and ears open. Stay safe. We'll be back as soon as possible."

He squeezed Kat's hand. She smiled at him encouragingly. She didn't feel like smiling. When Indra and Arthur walked away, she felt alone. Why did it have to be them to go? Couldn't someone else's husband walk into danger? She had grown to consider Indra part of the family. Barely even knew the girl, but the end of the world tends to speed things up.

Everyone looked around expectantly. Someone had to take charge, even while they were waiting. To her surprise, a young blonde wheeled himself to the front. He rolled to her side, grinned. "I'm Achim. You must be Arthur's wife. A pleasure."

Perplexed, it took her a moment to respond. She grabbed his hand, shook it. "Kat, nice to meet you."

He turned to the waiting group. "Okay, everyone. You heard the man. Let's sit down, get some rest. There isn't much protection from the elements here, but we'll be fine. Get some water, a snack. Arthur, Indra, Nicholas, and Sven—they'll be back in no time."

She ushered the children to the wall that separated the car lanes from the pedestrian walk way. It wasn't much, but it offered a little shade. They sat with their backs against the wall. She handed each of her children an apple.

"I don't want a stupid apple," Ron complained.

Erin folded her arms. "Me neither. Apples are dumb. I want food."

Grumpy. She was surprised they had lasted this long. Exhaustion darkened the mood. Her kids were used to a good life. Three square meals. Air-conditioning. A pool in the back-yard. She wouldn't say they were spoiled—she and Arthur had always worked hard to prevent that, but she had to admit they didn't know hardship. She had expected them to be grumpy sooner.

"Would you prefer a candy bar?" she asked, not in the mood for parenting.

When they didn't object, she handed them a bar each. They ate their chocolate in silence, emptied another bottle of water. Kat bit into an apple. To her, fruit would always be preferable to sweets. The juice spread through her mouth, better than any candy. She barely removed her eyes from the end of the bridge. Arthur, Indra, and the two men—she had already forgotten their names again—had vanished from sight a while ago. They'll be back soon, she reassured herself.

Achim checked on everyone. First, Kat and her family. They didn't need him. He moved on to a Mexican family—or so he guessed from the Spanish they spoke when he walked up. The daughter was crying. Just tired, the mother assured him. Most groups were the same. Exhaustion, tiredness, lack of sleep. Nothing serious.

He halted when he heard a sniff. A boy, maybe ten. Alone.

"Are you okay?" he asked. Big blue eyes looked up at him. Tears welled up in them. No answer. "Where's your mom? Your dad?"

The boy looked away. Still no answer.

"Are you alone?"

The boy shook his head, black hair bobbing. "She'll catch up soon."

Achim's heart stopped. He looked past the group. Everyone was sitting leisurely. Helga, the old lady he had gotten to know at the center, brought up the rear, as she had the whole night. She sat on her walker, sipped on a bottle of water, and chatted with a girl close to her.

"Where are they?"

The boy pointed to the end of the bridge. "Mom was tired," he explained. "She lay down for a nap. She'll catch up soon."

"Come on," he said with what he hoped was a casual voice. "I want to introduce you to someone."

The boy hesitated, but got up. Together, they made their way back to the front. "Kat, this young man here is waiting for his parents. I thought he might like to stay with your children while I check on his parents."

Kat searched his face. "What's your name?" The boy stayed silent. "That's okay. You don't have to tell me. I'm Kat. And these are Ron and Erin. Would you like a chocolate bar?"

She patted the ground in front of her. The boy sat down. "Ron, can you get him some chocolate from my pack?"

She got up, asked Achim quietly, "Where are his parents?"

He explained, "He says his mom was tired and lay down for a nap."

"Do we know how long ago this was, how far behind?"

Achim shook his head. "I have a feeling she won't catch up. I'll try and find out more from the group. Maybe someone saw something."

"There were twenty-one of us when we last counted," Kat added.

Achim did a quick headcount. Twenty-one. Everyone was here. Where were the boy's parents?

Carefully, he asked a few people in the group if they knew who the boy had been with. No one had seen anything. Helga confirmed she had been the last in the group since they set out at the mall. Before the coyotes, after the coyotes, she had brought up the rear.

For now, there was nothing he could do. He returned to Kat and the children. A questioning look from Kat. He didn't have to respond. She could see it in his face. He turned to the boy—Samuel, as Kat explained. "Do you remember when your mommy got tired?"

Samuel took his last bite from the chocolate bar, took his time chewing. "When we met the dogs. She told me to go on ahead with the group. She said she would catch up. She looked really, really tired."

Achim was sure the woman hadn't stayed behind for a nap. Something told him, the woman had been injured. She couldn't go on, wanted to give her son the best chance. And the brave little boy had walked on alone.

Kat and Achim exchanged another glance. He knew she understood. She knew the boy's mother was likely dead. "You can stay with us until your mom gets here," she declared. She wasn't ready to burst the bubble. Not here. Not now. They had to get to the hub first. She would tell him the truth. Just not yet.

CHAPTER
FIVE

The marina lay eerily empty. Not a soul around. No cars, no vehicles, nothing. They quickly reached the landing for the hubs. Each was covered like the gates to airplanes. They rushed from landing gate to landing gate just to find them empty. No ships. Not even a damn canoe. No way out.

"Here," cried Indra from ahead. Arthur caught up. A boat. A fucking boat. In the very last boat house. And people. Arthur had never been so happy to see people. Three men, all military, hustled around the boat. When they heard them approach, their eyes widened in shock. A weapon was raised. "Stay where you are."

Arthur raised his arms. A gesture of peace. "We are not here to harm you," he said calmly. "We came here from Center CBD One. Our group is waiting at the bridge. The shuttle bus didn't arrive, so we walked. We felt it would be better not to miss the transfer to the hub."

He was surprised they let him finish. The men looked too shocked to interrupt. No more routine. They hadn't expected them.

Man 1 turned to Man 2. "They said there wouldn't be anyone else."

Man 2 shrugged. "Looks like they were wrong."

Man 3 interrupted them. "I'll check with Houston." He turned to Arthur, Indra, and the two men with them. "Stay there. Don't do anything stupid."

He rushed off and into a cabin at the end. Arthur didn't move, didn't even dare look at one of the others. He just stood there, arms raised, and waited. When Man 3 came back, he nodded. "Houston says to follow protocol."

Arthur tensed. Protocol. "What does that mean?" he asked.

"Get your group here. Those who are registered to move into the hub will join the final shuttle." When Arthur didn't move, he added, "Come on, move. Hurry up. We were about to move out."

Arthur glanced at the sky. It was barely past noon. "I thought you left at sundown."

Man 1 shook his head. "Change of plans. They are speeding up the last transfer."

Something told Arthur that was as much information as he would get. He turned and walked back up the ramp. Indra walked next to him. The other two followed. When they were sure to be out of earshot from the landing, Indra turned to Arthur. "Something is wrong."

Arthur shared her feelings. He was sure something was wrong. "We don't have a choice."

"We could stay," Indra suggested half-heartedly. She knew from the news reports before the evacuation had started that there wouldn't be much time left on the surface. They didn't have a choice. Being able to choose her fate had always been important to her. Not having a choice made her feel trapped, tricked, cheated. She almost resented the hubs and the possibility of a new life there for the mere fact that she didn't have a choice. "There's always a choice. But I agree, in this case, there's no good one."

"We'll have to trust them." She snorted. "I don't like it either."

Indra worked hard to calm herself on the way back. Children had a way of picking up if something was wrong. Erin and Ron had been through enough. They should start their new lives with confidence, not worry.

Breath in. Two. Three. Four.

Breath out. Two. Three. Four.

She repeated the exercise every few minutes for the whole way. When they reached the bridge, she had tricked her body into calming. Her mind still raced, but she managed to control her body. She had to stay calm, strong. The children needed her.

Achim rolled toward them as soon as they came into view. "We've got another problem."

"What is it?" Arthur asked immediately.

"A boy, Samuel. He is alone. From what he said, we think his mother was injured in the coyote attack and told him to go on without her. He thinks she was tired and will catch up. Kat is looking after him for now." He rattled all this off very fast.

Arthur nodded. "Good. Kat's good with kids. We've got bigger fish to fry, I'm afraid."

A boy without a mother, and they didn't have time to deal with it. Indra swallowed the stinging sensation. "Thanks, Achim. I'll help Kat with the children."

Arthur thanked her, then explained to Achim that they had to gather everyone and get to the harbor, stat. Achim and Arthur hadn't even been introduced, yet Arthur knew he could rely on the boy. He had the same air of fight about him as Indra. He had noticed him earlier at the rear of the group. A spirit this heat and exhaustion couldn't crush was worth having around.

Without another word, they rushed to join the group. Within minutes, everyone was back on their feet for their final spurt. Our last steps on the surface of Earth, Indra thought. To her surprise, she didn't feel sad. Excitement overshadowed exhaustion. She was ready.

Erin and Ron accepted Samuel into their middle without question or objection. Ron understood more than the adults thought, more than Samuel. He knew the boy's mother wouldn't catch up. Just like he now knew that the bodies in the streets hadn't been sleeping. He was no little boy anymore. Erin might still be a dumb-dumb, but he wasn't.

He tried to distract Samuel with talk about video games and favorite books. They chattered animatedly all the way down to the water. He peered in when they walked past the boat garages—or whatever you would call those—and out onto the ocean beyond. Two men stood outside the last garage. Soldiers like those that had been everywhere when they had left home. He missed home. Samuel had never played his favorite video game. It would be fun to take him home and teach him. But he wasn't dumb. He knew they couldn't go back. He had heard that important dude talk at the center. No one could go home.

His father walked at the front again. He was the first to reach the soldiers. He couldn't hear what was said, but his father walked back toward them and explained that everyone needed to be identified before they could get onto the boat. His mother led them to the side, where they stood with his father. His father looked worried.

Arthur didn't know why, but he couldn't shake the feeling that something was wrong. He kissed Erin, smiled when she snuggled into his neck. The girl was tired. It had been a long week—weeks if he was honest. Everything had been chaotic since they left home.

He watched as the soldiers scanned the forearms of person after person. Passports had been replaced by chips implanted into the body a couple of decades ago. Supposedly, they were harder to fake. Arthur didn't believe it, but it didn't matter. The good thing was that they couldn't be lost.

The elderly woman who had brought up the rear most of the time stepped forward.

"ID." *Beep.* "Clear."

The line vanished through the gate until only Indra, Samuel, and Arthur's family were left. They had made it.

"ID," the soldier repeated. Now that they were back to procedure, he had the same monotone as the soldiers on evacuation day.

Arthur shifted Erin around, held out his left forearm. *Beep-Beep-Beep.*

The soldier scanned again. *Beep-Beep-Beep.*

"I'm afraid we can't read your chip."

Kat stepped up next to him. "Try again."

Beep-Beep-Beep.

"Sir, we will be unable to admit you without identification. Do you carry alternative identification?"

Arthur's heart raced. Alternative identification. No one carried those. The chips were supposed to be reliable. "Only my work ID."

"Do you work for a government facility, sir? Military?"

He didn't have his military ID on him. He had left the army a long time ago. He shook his head.

"We won't be able to admit you without identification. Please step aside."

Kat looked frantic. "Sir, this is my husband. I can vouch for him. He was sorted into the same city his whole family was. This is his daughter, his son."

"We can't admit anyone without identification."

"Then scan him again, for fuck's sake." Anger tinted Kat's voice.

Under Kat's glare, the soldier raised the scanner again. *Beep-Beep-Beep.*

He knew what to do. There was no other way. "Kat, it's okay. Go. I'll find a way to join you."

Kat's eyes welled with tears now. "I won't go without you. We'll all stay."

He turned to Indra. "Help her with the children, please."

Indra nodded. "I'll keep them safe—all of them." She knew there was no point arguing. She had felt something would go wrong, as it always did. She just hated that it had to be Arthur. Kat would need her. She had to be strong. For Kat. For the children. She swallowed the tears that threatened to spill, blinked. "I promise."

Kat shook her head. "I won't leave without you. We belong together."

Arthur's voice shook. "I'll find you. I promise. I need to know you are safe." He handed Erin to Indra, took his wife's face into both his hands. "I love you, Kat." He kissed her, put all his love into it. His heart tore in his chest. "I love you. I'll find you."

Kat held him tight. "Don't go."

He hugged her, kissed her cheek. "I have to. They won't let me go with you. I will find a way."

"Promise you'll come for us," Kat whispered. He dug his face into her hair. The smell of lavender filled his nostrils. He had always loved the smell of her hair. "I promise."

Letting go of her was the hardest thing he ever did.

He hugged both of his children. "Be a good boy, Ron. You are the man of the household now. Take care of your sister. Take care of your mom for me, okay?"

Ron was fighting tears. He wouldn't cry. He was a man. Unable to speak, he nodded.

"Erin, my baby girl." He kissed his daughter, who was still in Indra's arms.

"I love you, all of you."

Kat hugged him again. "I love you." A last kiss. No, not their last. He would find her again. "I love you, too."

He had been wrong. Letting go of her again was the hardest thing he ever did.

"Go, now. Be safe."

He held Kat's hand while the soldier scanned his family and Indra. *Beep. Beep. Beep. Beep.* One beep each. They were safe. When Kat's grip slipped from his, when they vanished from view, he collapsed against the wood outside. The soldier lingered for a moment. "I'm sorry, sir. It's not my decision. Protocol." And without waiting for a response, he stepped through the door, closed it behind him. Arthur was alone.

Indra had to guide Kat down the ramp. She carried Erin. Ron held his mother's other hand. Silent tears streamed down his face, despite his look of determination. Indra hated that he had to be strong. He was a child. He should be allowed weakness. Erin didn't understand what was happening. She would soon enough.

Samuel followed them at a trot. He looked confused. "Where's my mommy?"

Kat sobbed. She didn't have the strength to tell him. Helpless, she looked at Indra. "Let's get onto the boat, and then we'll see if we can find her, okay?"

She hated herself for lying to him—even told herself it wasn't *really* a lie, fully aware semantics didn't make it any less wrong. She just couldn't deal with the boy right now. Not while Kat and the children needed her. A few weeks ago, she had been on her own, fending for herself. Just herself. Now people were relying on her. She wouldn't let them down.

She had made a promise.

The boat swayed when they stepped on. A soldier showed them inside and to their seats. Besides their group, there were only ten or so other people, all of them military types. Achim assisted one of them in attaching his wheelchair to the boat. It reminded her of taking the bus into downtown. She had never been on a boat before.

She was separated from Kat by Erin, Ron, and Samuel, so there was no way for her to comfort the woman. Kat rested her head against the window behind, eyes closed. Tears streamed down her face. Indra fought her own tears. None of this seemed fair. They were supposed to be on the way to a new life, an underwater hub. Underwater, for fuck's sake. She would live underwater like a fucking dolphin. But none of it seemed to matter. Arthur. Samuel's mother. All the people they had lost. Too much sacrifice. Earth was dying, and they cared about a fucking ID not scanning. What did one person matter?

None of it was fair.

As they rocked toward their destination, Kat calmed, her pain numbed. She leaned down and kissed her son's head. Smiled at her daughter. She couldn't fall apart. She was a mother. Her children came first.

Arthur would find them again. She believed it—had to believe it—with all her heart.

Their boat landed at a platform in the middle of nowhere. Nothing but ocean around. It reminded her of the oil platforms off the coast. Metal beams. Sea lions. Birds. She pointed the sea lions out to her children. Erin squealed with delight. "Can I go pet them?"

Even Ron pressed his face against the window.

While Indra explained to Erin that the sea lions didn't like cuddles and distracted her daughter with fun facts about sea lions: "Did you know that sea lions look a lot like true seals, but you can tell them apart by their ears?" She looked out onto the wide ocean. Somewhere out there was her husband. She watched the waves. Up. Down. Up. Down.

"Follow me," a soldier said and waited by the door. They shouldered their luggage and stepped out into the bright sun. It wasn't as hot out here with the ocean cooling the air, but she still felt sweat beads again within seconds.

Two soldiers handed her the cart she had used to drag her children at the bottom of a ramp. She accepted it with a nod. Erin climbed in immediately. Samuel eyed the cart jealously. "You can climb in, too, if you like," Indra offered. Samuel smiled and climbed onto the cart. He seemed to have forgotten about his mother for the moment—or maybe he didn't dare ask again. She would talk to him. Soon.

Achim stayed with Helga. A soldier assisted her down the ramp, where they returned her walker. Excitement ran through the group. They had made it. They were safe. He looked around, found Indra with Kat, her children, and Samuel. Samuel rode in the cart with Erin, already seemed to belong. And then he noticed that Arthur was nowhere to be seen. He had assumed he was in a different part of the boat. He slowed until they caught up with him. When he opened his mouth, Indra shook her head. "Don't ask," she mouthed. He swallowed his question, instead merely joined them on the way down the platform.

Another pair of soldiers waited by a door. A small building stood in the middle of the platform, merely more than a garden shed. A small cube with nothing but a door. The doors slid open and revealed an elevator. Their group gathered in front.

"The elevator will bring you to the lower level, where you will board the submarine. The elevator carries six people at a time. The submarine carries four. Please be patient while groups are transported down to the waiting area and from there into the city."

Achim was sick of the voice in which the soldiers talked. No intonation, like a song with only one note. He hoped people in the city were less—he searched for the right word—scripted. Robotic?

Helga swayed slightly in the heat. Achim rushed to her side, steadied her with a hand. "You should go first." He raised his voice. "Is it cooler down there?"

The soldier glanced at him, confirmed.

"It's too hot up here. The elderly and children should get out of the sun."

The soldier stared at Achim, torn between agreeing with a child—Achim was nothing else in his eyes—and the fact that the child was right. In the end, he agreed. "Ma'am," he said as he pointed at the woman next to the boy in the wheelchair. "Please step onto the elevator." He scanned the group, pointed to those with babies, and instructed the mothers to join the old lady. The door closed and the first group vanished.

Kat and the children went next, with another mother carrying a baby in a sling. Achim wiped sweat from his brow. The midday sun burnt mercilessly from above. "I can't wait to get out of the heat," he panted.

Indra looked out onto the ocean. "I'm not so sure. This might be the last time we see the sun."

Achim hadn't thought about it. Not like that. Since he had been evacuated, it had been day to day—fuck, even hour to hour while they walked. He had been so set on getting to the under-water city that he hadn't considered the consequences. If the earth's surface would soon be unfit for living, they would spend the rest of their lives under the surface.

"But we'll be alive," he stated.

Indra smiled. "Yes, we'll be alive." Her eyes were still fixed on the horizon. After a long pause, she added, "I've always loved the ocean."

Achim watched her. "Now you'll get to live in it. You'll be a beautiful mermaid."

They both laughed.

When the elevator returned for them, they stepped on. The ride down was humid, and it felt like there wasn't enough air in the small metal coffin. Achim hated small spaces. He had to force himself to breathe.

The door opened, and they emerged onto another platform, just above the water's surface, and Achim wondered why the boat hadn't just released them on the lower level, instead making them climb up the ramp to take the elevator. A breeze blew past, dried some of their sweat. The ceiling blocked the sun and made the temperature bearable. A small group gathered next to another landing gate. They joined them and found a yellow submarine hovering next to the dock. The hatch was closed and sealed and shortly after, it disappeared into the blue. He leaned over the edge of the platform, watched it as long as possible.

Indra smiled. A submarine. It had been a dream of hers to dive in a submarine one day. She had never thought it would actually happen. It had been a dream on the "Things that seem impossible, but a girl can dream" list. Now, she was minutes from entering a submarine—a yellow submarine, just like in the *Beatles* song.

"A submarine," she stammered, and Achim looked up at her. "A real submarine."

"Would you come down with me? I'm not too good with small spaces." She could tell it cost him a lot to admit it. She placed on hand on his shoulder. "I'll be there. That's what friends are for."

A glint flickered through his eyes. She couldn't place it. Then it was gone and he smiled. "Thank you!"

"It will be our little adventure," she added.

"Our little adventure," he repeated.

Indra joined Kat, made sure the woman was okay. She would take the submarine with the children, hers and Samuel. Achim had left her to check on Helga, the elderly woman with the walker. She seemed nervous at the sight of the submarine.

"See you on the flip side," she said with a grin when Kat and the children climbed through the hatch.

"See you soon."

She stood by the side of the dock and followed the submarine into the depth until it was nothing more than a shadow. Even then, she kept her gaze on the spot where it had been, her thoughts with the family under the waves. She wondered what would happen to Arthur, hoped he would get to keep his promise.

Achim pulled her from her thoughts by taking her hand. "They'll be okay."

She tore her eyes from the deep blue. "I hope so."

The submarine returned for the next group, and the next, until only Indra, Achim, and Helga were left. Achim had insisted that the woman travel with them, to keep her company. "Did you know each other—you know—before?" Indra asked. Achim shook his head. "Met her at the center. She was alone, so was I. She's a lovely woman."

Helga smiled at the compliment. "And you are quite the lovely young lad. If I were your age, I'd ask you on a date."

They laughed. It made some of the worry fall way.

When the submarine returned for them, two soldiers helped lower Achim through the hatch. Indra had expected him to be embarrassed. Instead, he cheered them on and laughed through the procedure. His wheelchair lay folded in a corner, as they carried him onto one of the passenger seats.

"Buckle up, everyone," one of the soldiers instructed. The

other climbed back out of the hatch. He'd be on the last shuttle down, along with some of the service personnel.

Indra leaned against the wall and turned to look out into the blue. The waves crashed against the window, which sat half submerged. Beeps and commands came from the captain—was that what you called a submarine diver? "Ready for departure."

Slowly, the water level rose against the window. She didn't even get a last glance at the sun before they vanished under the surface. They sank. And sank. Enveloped in deep blue, the outside grew darker and darker.

They sank further, leveled. Darkness crept by outside, the occasional glimpse of a fish, as they neared their destination.

All of them gasped when the city came into view. A glittering bubble in the distance. A snow globe under the ocean's surface, a hope for home.

CHARACTERS

Following is a list of the characters in this book. Read at your own discretion, as they might contain minor spoilers. I always found the character descriptions in classic plays more than helpful when I forgot who characters were, so I decided to include something similar.

Achim: A young man in a wheelchair who travels with the group to Long Beach.

Arthur Reid: Arthur is 36 when the story starts. He is married to Kathryn Jane Reid and father to Ronald Dean and Erin Ann Reid.

Dana: Volunteer at the center.

Erin Ann Reid: Erin is 7 when the story starts and the daughter of Arthur and Kat.

Helga: An old woman with a walker who travels with the group to Long Beach.

Indra Banks: She is 18 when the story starts. Her family is not part of the story.

Jim Washington: One of the men who travel with the group to Long Beach.

Kathryn Jane Reid: Kat is 33 when the story starts. She is married to Arthur Reid and mother to Ronald Dean and Erin Ann Reid.

Nicholas: One of the men who crosses the bridge with Arthur.

Ronald Dean Reid: Ron is 10 when the story starts and the son of Arthur and Kat.

Samuel: The kid who lost his mother to the coyotes.

Sven: One of the men who crosses the bridge with Arthur.

Tinkerbell: The cat of the Reid family.

THANK YOU

Thank you for buying this book. It means the world to me.

I'm an independent author and publishing my books came with ups and downs. When I published my first book, Chase, I hired an editor, spent thousands of dollars on getting my books beta-read, copy-edited, and line-edited, but many issues remained unseen. There were errors on the covers I had commissioned with a professional cover designer, and a marketing expert messed up the advertising, costing me more money without getting my books to people who would enjoy the stories. I made many mistakes, but I also learned a lot.

Telling stories is what I do best, what gives me joy, and I couldn't do it without you: the reader of this story. Thank you again.

WANT MORE?

Find more information about my published and upcoming novels, as well as my podcast and essays about sustainability, biodiversity, and living a life worth living on my website: katehildenbrand.com

SUPPORT KATE

Writing, editing, and publishing books, creating written and video episodes, and everything else that goes into spreading my words is a lot of work. Your support means everything. Thank you!

katehildenbrand.com/support

ABOUT THE AUTHOR

Kate has been reading and writing for as long as she can remember. As a child she could be found cooped up in armchairs, snuggled in beds, or propped inside doorframes reading books like *The Little Prince* and *The Diary of a Young Girl*—despite being a bit younger than the target audience.

During a summer vacation at her grandmother's house, she wrote her first story about a cigarette going on an adventure to avoid death by fire. This morbidly fun tale was inspired by her grandmother's chain-smoking habits.

Reading a poem at her best friend's funeral as a teenager made her realize just how much power words hold.

With the help of Moony, Wormtail, Padfoot, and Prongs, as well as Bilbo, Frodo, Pippin, and the like, she wrote fantasy novels and short stories. One of her first finished books—and possibly the most embarrassing part of her writing career—was a sequel to Tolkien's *The Lord of the Rings*.

It was years before she moved on to original work and even longer before any of it had much value. In 2015, she wrote Chase, an adult dystopian, during NaNoWriMo—well, a very rough first draft. After a long four years, it is finally edited and ready for you to read.

BOOKS BY KATE BREUER

THE WILLOW SERIES

How far will a mother go to protect her daughter? What dangers will a son risk to defy his father within a system of evil?

The city is a well-ordered one. Those in the inner rings control the world. Those outside the center do as they are told…without question. Questions. You can die for asking the wrong question.

Chase's daughter, Willow, like every other child, is the 'Property of the State.' Usually, so long as you keep your head down, the 'State' pays no attention, and parents raise their children as they always have. Unfortunately, the state has a profound interest in 5-year-old Willow. Chase needs to protect her little girl - but there is nowhere to run, nowhere to hide.

Nate is a son of the inner circle. As the son of the city's leading man, Nate is expected to do his duty and 'keep the peace' as an officer of the state. His reward? To rise, like his father, to the mayorship of the city.

Nate discovers that 'keeping the peace' involves torture, murder, and unspeakable crimes. This is his heritage. This is the city that he will one day rule.

When their worlds collide, Nate will hold the fate of Chase and Willow in his hands. Will he have the courage to rebel? Can he save Willow from her inevitable fate?

THE WATER & EARTH SERIES

Spores

Heat, Waves, Darkness, and Storm – planned

When the surface of the earth becomes uninhabitable, humans flee underneath the oceans. Well, those who are lucky enough to get into the utopia. Many are left fighting for limited living space in cave systems created by the last large earthquake in the San Andreas fault. Those who didn't get into the bubble cities live alongside those who didn't uphold the high standards of the society.

STANDALONE WORKS

Out of Hiding

When a group of dark wizards kills magicians and non-magicians alike, magicians are forced out of hiding after thousands of years of peaceful coexistence. Soon after, magic on one side and weapons on the other create a bloody match and a war seems unavoidable. Trying to prevent a genocide, Cassandra sets out to prove magicians are not a threat. It's the fight of a witch who is overwhelmed with daily life against a society who is just as eager to hunt witches as it was in the middle ages. She finds new friends and reunites with old ones along the way – prominently among them a gay dwarf and a dragon breeder with a drinking problem.

CHILDREN'S BOOKS

You Can Do It, Squirrel!

Also available in German, German-English bilingual, and English-German bilingual versions.